This

Little Princess™

Annual belongs to

Name: _Jannie ♥_

Age: _7_

Contents

Say Hello To Little Princess	Page 6
Little Princess	Page 7
Gilbert and Algie	Page 8
Puss, Scruff and Horace	Page 9
King and Queen	Page 10
Maid, Chef and General	Page 11
Gardener, Prime Minister and Admiral	Page 12
Great Uncle Walter, Great Auntie, Auntie and Baby Cousin	Page 13
Crown Crisis	Page 14
Colouring: Little Princess	Page 15
Story: I Want My Robin	Page 16
Make Your Own Bird Feeder	Page 26
Shadow Spot	Page 28
Royal Writing	Page 29
Perfect Match	Page 30
Make Your Own Crown	Page 31
Smells Yummy, Looks Yummy	Page 32
Washday Wordsearch	Page 34
Pirate Grid Picture	Page 35
Royal Invitation	Page 36
Make Your Own Special Occasion Wellies	Page 38
Gymkhana Chaos	Page 40
Colouring: Gardener	Page 41
Story: I Want To Go On Holiday	Page 42
Holiday!	Page 52
When I Grow Up	Page 54
Biscuit Detective	Page 55
Ready Or Not	Page 56
Dot To Dot	Page 58
Toy Box Total	Page 59
King Of The Castle	Page 60
Prime Minister Puzzle	Page 62
I Didn't Do It	Page 63
Dressing Up Day	Page 64
Who Wants To Play	Page 66
Royal Rewards	Page 67
Story: I Want To Recycle	Page 68
Make Your Own Desk Tidy	Page 78
Admiral's Pond Puzzler	Page 80
Algie's Brainteaser Challenge	Page 81
The A To Z Of The Little Princess	Page 82
Colouring: Fairground	Page 86
My Best Things	Page 88
Suppertime Squares	Page 90
Castle Close-ups	Page 91
Colouring: Little Princess, Gilbert, Puss and Scruff	Page 92
Answers	Page 93

Published 2013. Century Books Ltd.
Unit 1, Upside Station Building Solsbro Road,
Torquay, Devon, UK, TQ26FD

books@centurybooksltd.co.uk

centum

Say Hello To Little Princess

Welcome to the Little Princess Annual 2014!

Join Little Princess and her friends as she gets into mischief around the castle and in the grounds. There are lots of fun activities, games and stories for you to enjoy. So get ready to explore the castle too.

Little Princess is ready for her next adventure!

Colour in her picture as neatly as you can.

The castle is bursting with hidden goodies to discover. Count them up and write how many you find in each circle.

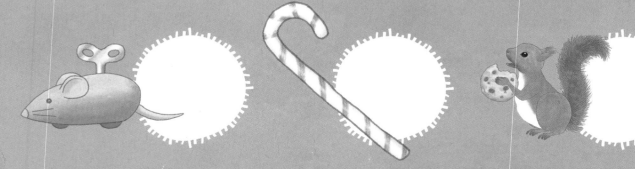

Little Princess

Little Princess is full of royal mischief and can't resist being a little cheeky from time to time. She can be a bit stubborn, but she knows when to put on a big smile and make everything better.

Little Princess is always ready to learn more about the world and how things work. She loves to have adventures and spends every day exploring the castle and grounds.

Write over Little Princess's name

Little Princess

Did you know?
Little Princess loves to dress up and has a superhero costume.

Gilbert

Gilbert is Little Princess's favourite teddy bear. He is always by her side and is ready to lend a hand with her wild ideas.

Write over Gilbert's name

Gilbert

Algie

Algie is Little Princess's best friend. He is great fun and loves to play jokes. He helps with her most exciting adventures, from hunting dragons to building tree houses.

Did you know?
Algie is the same age as the Little Princess — four years old.

Puss

Puss is a very clever cat. He is always there to assist Little Princess whether he wants to not. Puss is also best friends with Scruff, although he doesn't always like to admit it.

Scruff

Scruff is loyal like every good dog. He has as much energy as Little Princess and is very excitable, especially when bones are part of a plan.

Write over Puss and Scruff's names.

Puss and Scruff

Did you know?
Horace used to belong to Great Uncle Walter.

Horace

Horace is the newest member of Little Princess's animal gang. He is a Shetland pony who is as stubborn as Little Princess.

King

King is the best dad any little princess could wish for. He always has lots of helpful advice for Little Princess and he loves a game of croquet in the castle garden.

Queen

Queen is Little Princess's brilliant mum. She is always kind, even when Little Princess has done something a little bit silly. Queen has her breakfast in bed and her favourite food is ice cream, just like Little Princess.

Write over King and Queen's names.

King and Queen

Maid

Maid is always kind and good-humoured, even when Little Princess's bedroom is a mess. She does lots of jobs around the castle and is not afraid to be a bit bossy. Maid doesn't like her clean washing getting muddy!

Chef

Chef is always cooking up tasty treats for Little Princess and the rest of the castle. Like all good chefs he can sometimes be grumpy. But most of the time he doesn't mind Little Princess 'helping' in the royal kitchen.

General

General is always there to give Little Princess a helping hand. He doesn't go anywhere without his trusty hobbyhorse, Nessie. General isn't as brave as you might expect, but he always does his best.

Gardener

Gardener knows everything about nature and the outdoors and he teaches Little Princess all the best bits. He grows lots of interesting vegetables including princess-shaped potatoes

Prime Minister

Prime Minister is a playful politician who likes to zoom around the castle on his tricycle. He enjoys all Little Princess's cheeky games — even mud-pie-throwing contests.

Admiral

Admiral is in charge of the royal fleet of toy boats. He likes to be close at hand and stays in the castle pond. He is very funny and Little Princess can count on him to join in games like fishing for sea monsters!

Little Princess has lots of royal relations who visit the castle and join in her adventures.

Great Uncle Walter

Great Uncle Walter loves a party almost as much as he loves adventures. He is a world-famous explorer. Great Uncle Walter's cockatoo, Claptrap, never leaves his side.

Did you know?
Great Uncle Walter discovered the world's tallest tree and climbed it!

Great Auntie

Great Auntie enjoys visiting the castle and always likes a kiss from Little Princess, whether she wants to give one or not!

Auntie and Baby Cousin

Auntie is the Queen's sister. She comes to visit with her son, Baby Cousin, who is even messier than Little Princess.

Crown Crisis

Little Princess has left her crown in the castle garden!
Help her through the maze to rescue it. Watch out for
wildlife and hazards blocking the way.

Colouring: Little Princess

Little Princess is searching for presents in the castle. Use crayons or pencils to colour in the picture.

How many presents can you see?

15

I Want My Robin

It was a chilly day in the castle garden, and Little Princess was hiding in a bush.

"I'm birdy watching," she said.

She looked up into the trees.

"Ooo there's a wild birdy, a red one!" cried Little Princess.

The red bird was called a robin.

"HELLO," she bellowed.

But she was so loud that the robin was startled and flew away.

The robin landed next to Gardener, who was planting cauliflowers.

"Oh hello, Little Princess. What's the trouble?"

"I'm trying to watch the robin," she explained. "But he won't sit still!"

"Aha," said Gardener with a smile. "You need some camouflage."

"Camel – what?" asked Little Princess.

"Camouflage," Gardener explained. "You dress up to look like the things around you. Then the robin won't know you're there!"

Little Princess waited in her camouflage.

The robin came nearer and nearer.

"Hello!" called Little Princess.

But she was still too noisy! The robin flew away again.

"Nice camouflage," called Gardener.

"But you're not supposed to see me!" she cried.

"Ahoy there, Princess." Admiral shouted from his pond.

"Yoo hoo, Princess." General cried from the sandpit.

"Hello, Princess." Prime Minister called from the swing.

Little Princess's camouflage didn't fool anyone.

"What's the use of this camel-stuff if everyone can see me?" she asked Gardener.

"What you need is a hide," he said. "A secret place to watch birds from."

"Oooh, I like secrets," said Little Princess.

Gardener took the Little Princess to the shed.

"But this is just the shed!" she cried.

Gardener chuckled.

"That is what the birds will think too," he said. "And if you keep nice and quiet, they won't know you're inside."

Inside the shed, the Gardener propped the window open and hung up some seed to attract the robin.

"Remember, you must stay nice and quiet," he told Little Princess.

"Oh yes, must be quiet," Little Princess whispered. "I'm going to ask him in for tea."

"No, no, no, you mustn't do that," cried Gardener. "He's a wild bird, not a pet."

Gardener shut the door and left Little Princess to do some birdy watching.

After a while Little Princess sighed.

"All I've seen is some black birdies," she said in a sad voice.

Just then the robin landed on the seed and began to eat!

"My robin!" cried Little Princess.

Little Princess was so excited to see the robin, she forgot what Gardener had told her.

"Would you like to come in for tea?" she whispered to the robin.

She reached up for the watering can, which was on the highest shelf.

CRASH!

Everything from the shelves fell in a heap and the window crashed shut. The robin was trapped inside!

"Oh no," cried Little Princess.

The robin was afraid. He flew around the shed in circles.

Little Princess frowned.

"I don't think he's happy," she said. "I'm sorry, Robin, Gardener was right, you should be outside with your friends."

She opened the door and tried to set the robin free. But he was too scared and hid in a flowerpot.

"Seen any birds yet?" Gardener asked Little Princess.

Just then the robin wooshed out of the shed.

"My shed!" cried Gardener when he saw the mess.

Little Princess's bottom lip started to quiver.

"He came in, but he didn't like it, so I tried to let him out," she said. "But ... but ... I'm sorry!"

She began to cry.

"There, there, Princess," said Gardener with a smile. "He's all right now."

The robin was sitting on a branch singing happily. Gardener looked into the shed.

"It looks like we have a little job to do here," he said.

Little Princess grabbed a broom and began to sweep.

"Are you sure there was just one robin in here?" said Gardener with a chuckle. "It looks like he had quite a party!"

Little Princess decided to try birdy watching again.

"All the birdies are staying outside today," she said with a grin.

Make Your Own Bird Feeder

You will need:

Pinecone (open)
String
Peanut butter
Birdseed mix
Bowl

You can make your own birdfeeder and try birdy watching just like Little Princess. Just follow the instructions below.

Ask a grown-up to hang your bird feeder securely.

Instructions:

1. Tie a string around the pinecone.
2. Use a spoon (or your fingers!) to spread the peanut butter onto the pinecone. Make sure to get the mixture into the open areas of the pinecone.
3. Place birdseed in the bowl. Roll the pinecone covered in sticky peanut butter in seed until it is well covered.
4. Hang your pinecone feeder outside.

Look out for these feathered friends visiting your feeder:

Get ready to get messy! Wear an apron and ask a grown-up to help with tricky parts.

Robin

Crow

Swallow

Shadow Spot

King has gathered everyone into the royal dining room to listen to his new music box. Draw lines to match King and his friends to their shadows.

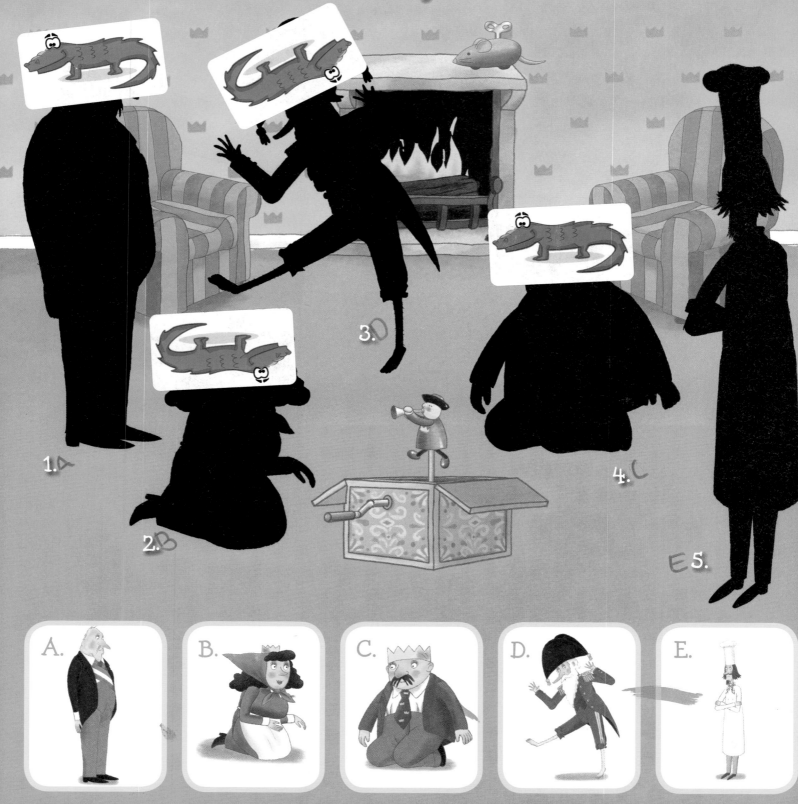

Royal  Writing

Little Princess is practising her writing. Can you help her solve these word problems?

1. Who's hiding?

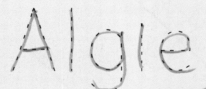 Algie

2. Unscramble the letters to reveal Little Princess's favourite food.

 g u s e a s a s

s a u s a g e s

3. Little Princess is playing with her doll today. How many times does the word 'doll' appear in this word square?

A	D	E	W	S
D	O	L	L¹	P
P	L	B	I	K
E	L³	R	Y	H
N	D	O	L	L²

Write your answer here: 3

A.

B.

C.

D.

E.

F.

G.

H.

Perfect Match

Everyone is going to the seaside and Little Princess has packed a lot of things to take. Look at these pairs of seaside treats. Which two match perfectly?

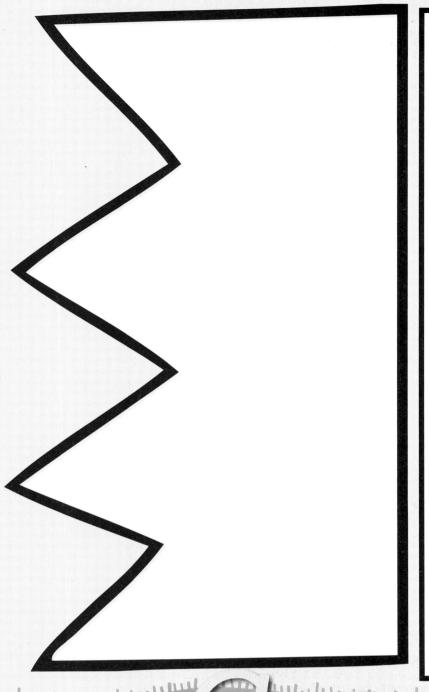

GLUE END

GLUE END

Make Your Own Crown

Every little princess or prince needs a crown. Now you can make your own! Just follow the instructions below.

You will need:
Card
Glue
Paint
Scissors

Remember scissors are sharp so ask a grown-up to help with cutting out.

Instructions:

1. Draw these shapes onto thick card.
2. Colour or paint the crown and headbands.
3. Ask a grown-up to cut out the pieces.
4. Glue one of the bands to one edge of the crown shape.
5. Glue the other edge of the headband to the crown.
6. Fit the headband around your head and trim off the extra part.
7. The crown should fit on your head with the crown shape at the front.

Add some glitter to make your crown extra special.

31

Smells Yummy, Looks Yummy

Little Princess is helping Chef bake some tasty royal cupcakes in the kitchen. Ask a grown-up to help you make some too.

Ingredients:
- 125g self-raising flour
- 125g castor sugar
- 125g soft unsalted butter
- 2 eggs
- ½ tbsp vanilla extract
- 2 tbsp milk

For the icing:
- 300g icing sugar
- 2–3 tbsp water
- 12 glacé cherries

Get ready to get messy! Remember to wear an apron.

Stay Safe! Always ask a grown-up to help when using hot ovens, kitchen appliances or knives.

1. Ask a grown-up to preheat the oven to 200°C/400°F/Gas Mark 6.
2. Line a muffin tin with 12 cake cases.
3. Cream the butter and sugar together with a wooden spoon.
4. Beat in the eggs one at a time.
5. Slowly stir in the flour and the vanilla extract.
6. Add the milk a little at a time, until the mixture is smooth.
7. Use a spoon to divide the mixture between the 12 cake cases.
8. Ask a grown-up to place the muffin tin into the oven. Bake for 15–20 minutes or until the cakes are golden brown.
9. Cool the cakes in their cases on a wire rack.
10. To make the icing, sieve the icing sugar into a large bowl and stir in the water a little at a time, until the mixture is smooth.
11. When the cakes are cool, cover them in icing and put a glacé cherry on top.
12. Wait for the icing to harden – then tuck in!

Washday Wordsearch

Maid is doing lots of laundry today. See if you can find the name of each item of washing among the letters in the wordsearch grid. They are hiding down, across and diagonally.

K	Y	K	J	U	M	P	E	B	V
N	V	E	S	I	N	P	Y	S	B
I	S	S	Y	D	L	T	S	H	E
C	O	P	H	R	S	R	M	I	L
K	C	S	V	E	L	T	R	R	U
E	K	E	V	S	E	H	U	T	C
R	S	U	U	S	G	T	S	T	T
S	R	O	E	I	B	Q	A	A	G
V	B	Q	N	I	N	X	O	C	Y
T	F	D	T	X	R	C	Q	V	Q

COAT   SHEET
DRESS   SHIRT
JUMPER   SOCKS
KNICKERS   TROUSERS
NIGHTIE   VEST

Pirate
Grid Picture

Little Princess has decided to be a pirate so that she doesn't have to wash or do as she's told!

Use the grid to copy the picture square by square. Then use crayons or pencils to colour in your picture.

Royal Invitation

Little Princess has written to invite you to a secret party.
Some of the invitation is in code!
Use the picture key to find the missing words and see what the invitation says.

KEY

 Cake Gilbert Castle  Games Present Ice Cream

Dear ....

You are invited to an extra special secret

party at the .

, Puss and Scruff will be there too. If you

have a favourite teddy bear please bring it as well.

Then it can play with .

There will be lots of and scrummy

Chef is making a wobbly jelly as well.

I don't want too many people to come to

the party, in case they eat all the . That is why I

am writing in code. There will be lots of

balloons and 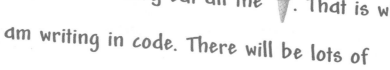.

If you like you can bring me a 🎁.

I look forward to seeing you at my party.

From,

Little Princess

Make Your Own
Special Occasion
Wellies

Get ready to get messy!
Ask a grown-up to help with cutting and sticking.

You will need:
Pair of old wellington boots
Fabric
Ribbon
Glitter
Double-sided tape
Safety scissors
Strong glue

e Princess ····· Little Princess

38

Instructions:

1. Make sure your wellingtons are clean and dry.
2. Ask a grown-up to cut out a rectangle of your fabric. It should measure 18cm by 15cm.
3. Stick a strip of double-sided tape horizontally across the centre of the rectangle.
4. Fold the fabric from the top and from the bottom and stick down along the double-sided tape.
5. Use some ribbon to make a loop and tie a knot to form a bow..
6. Trim off any excess ribbon.
7. Use glitter and glue to decorate your bow.
8. Ask a grown-up to stick your bows onto the front of your wellingtons with glue.

Stay Safe! Always ask a grown-up to help when using scissors and glue.

Wear your wellies to every special occasion.

Remember you will need to make two bows, one for each welly!

Princess • • • • • • • • Little Princess • • • • • • • • • Princess • • • • • Little Princess • • • • • • • • • Little P

39

Gymkhana Chaos

General has organised a gymkhana around the castle grounds. Who will win the cake – General on Nessie, Algie on his bike or Little Princess on Horace? Follow the tracks to see who will reach the cake.

Colouring: Gardener

Today Gardener is looking after his vegetable patch.
Use crayons or pencils to colour him in.

How many white rabbits
can you see?

5

Story:
I Want To Go On Holiday

Little Princess was in her bedroom when Maid came to the door.

"Princess, there's a postcard for you," said Maid.

"For me?" gasped Little Princess. "But I can't read it."

"Shall I take a look?" asked Maid helpfully.

The postcard was from Great Auntie, on holiday. She'd made sandcastles, sunbathed, had a donkey ride and, best of all, she ate ice cream – every day!

"I want to go on holiday too," squealed Little Princess.

Little Princess ran
to the dining room
where all the grown-ups
were cleaning.

"Daddy, can we go
on holiday like Great
Auntie?" she shouted.

"Not today," said King.
"Today's cleaning day."

"We can't go anywhere
until we've tidied,
cleaned and scrubbed
the castle from top to
bottom," added Queen.

Little Princess had a
brilliant idea. She ran to
her room.

"I've finished all my cleaning," announced Little Princess. "So I'm going on my own special seaside holiday with Desmond."

She grabbed Desmond, the inflatable crocodile, and packed some holiday things into her suitcase.

"We're off to the seaside!" Little Princess called to Maid as she headed outside.

Maid was dusting the royal portraits.

"It's all right for some," she huffed.

Little Princess arranged Desmond next to the pond.

"What a lovely blue sea!" she said.

She decided that the first thing she wanted to do on holiday was sunbathe.

Squelch. Skwerp. Little Princess covered herself in sun cream from head to toe.

"I'm bored of sunbathing now," she sighed after a minute. "Next, sightseeing!"

Sightseeing in the garden wasn't much fun.

"I've seen everything before," Little Princess grumbled.

Then an idea popped into her head.

"I'll have a donkey ride like Great Auntie," she said.

Little Princess thought that Desmond would make a perfect donkey.

"Gee up, Desmond, faster!" she squealed.

She bounced up and down so much that Desmond burst.

Little Princess decided to build sandcastles. But they kept falling down.

Then she heard laughter coming from the castle.

Little Princess went to investigate.

In the hall King, Queen and Prime Minister were cleaning and having fun.

"What's going on?" demanded Little Princess.

"Just working hard cleaning," King replied.

"Are you enjoying your holiday, sweetheart?" Queen asked Little Princess.

Little Princess didn't want to admit that cleaning looked more fun than holiday.

"Err, y-yes, I'm having lots of fun," she said.

Little Princess was shocked to find Chef and Maid having fun in the kitchen too.

"Aren't you glad you're not stuck inside with us, Princess?" called Maid as a bag of flour exploded all over Chef.

Little Princess decided that a nice holiday picnic would cheer her up.

She sat on her lilo and searched the picnic basket. Finally she found it.

"Ice cream!"

Little Princess hadn't learnt anything from Desmond bursting. She bounced up and down so hard that the lilo went POP!

Little Princess soared through the air.

"Aaagggh!"

Little Princess landed in a heap, covered in the picnic.

"I DON'T WANT TO BE ON HOLIDAY ANY MORE!" she yelled at the top of her voice.

"Neither do I," said an unexpected voice.

It was Great Auntie!

"I'd much rather be here with you," she said.

Little Princess beamed.

"I know!" she replied. "We can both NOT be on holiday together."

Inside, everyone had finally finished cleaning.

"I think we could all use a bit of a holiday," exclaimed King.

Everyone headed outside to the garden.

"Princess, Great Auntie, come and join us," called King.

Little Princess grinned at Great Auntie.

"I think we'd better," she said. "They won't enjoy themselves on their own!"

suitcase

picnic

camera

Holiday!

Write the names of these things
Little Princess is packing for her holiday.

sun cream

toothbrush

sunglasses

What would your dream holiday look like?
Use this space to draw a picture of it.

Try keeping a holiday scrapbook. Fill it with tickets, postcards and interesting food wrappers.

What are you going to pack? Draw the things you want to take in this suitcase.

When I Grow Up

Little Princess has lots of ideas about what she wants
to be when she grows up.
Sometimes she wants to be a vet and look after poorly animals.
Then she feels like being a policeman and making all the rules.
One day she'd like to be an astronaut and go to space.
And the next day she wants to be an explorer and
discover rare butterflies.
What would you like to be when you grow up?

Biscuit Detective

Someone has eaten all of Little Princess's freshly baked biscuits. Can you follow the trail of crumbs and help her to find the biscuit thief?

Ready or Not

Little Princess and her friends are playing an exciting
game of hide and seek in the castle grounds.

Help her to search for everyone hiding
in the picture.

Tick the boxes when you find them.

57

Dot to Dot

Join up the dots to show who General is taking for a teatime ride.

When you have finished the outline, use pencils or crayons to colour the picture in.

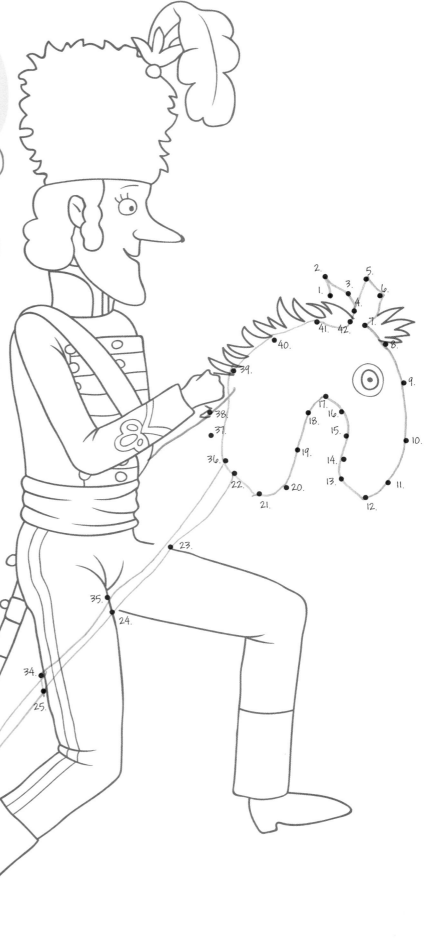

Toy Box Total

There are a lot of toys to keep track of in Little Princess's bedroom — especially when she doesn't want to tidy up.

Try these toy box sums and see how many toys you can count!

How many toy planes are there? 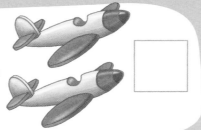 ☐

Now count the boats.  ☐

How many toys are there when you add the toy planes and boats together? ☐

Make these sets of crayons the same by drawing some in the second box.

 + 🧸 = ☐

King Of The Castle

Little Princess wants to play a game with you.
See who can avoid the hazards and reach the top
to be crowned King of the Castle!

How to play:

1. Ask up to three of your friends to play.

2. Decide which Little Princess character you want to be.

3. Put your counters at the start.

4. Take turns to throw the dice.

5. Start at number 1 and move your counter across the board row by row following the numbers.

6. If you land on a space with the bottom of a ladder in it, climb the ladder to the square at the top.

7. If you land on a space with the top of a slide in it, slide down it to the square at the bottom.

8. Follow the instruction if you land on a crown square.

9. The first player to reach number 24 is King of the Castle.

24

23

Horace to the rescue! Move forward 1 space.

21

17

18

19

Trip over Scruff. Back 2 spaces.

16

15

14

Time to tidy up. Back 1 space.

9

10

Stop for cake. Miss a turn.

12

Find Algie's bike. Move forward 2 spaces.

6

1

2

Wrong door. Miss a turn.

4

Prime Minister Puzzle

Prime Minister is oiling his tricycle wheels ready to race around the castle grounds.

Which is the missing puzzle piece?

1.

2.

3.

I Didn't Do It

Someone has made a mess in Chef's kitchen! Take a careful look at these two pictures. Can you circle five differences between them?

Dressing Up Day

Design and colour two
new costumes for
Little Princess
to wear.

Little Princess loves to dress up. She has lots of fun outfits to choose from in her dressing-up box, but she would love to have some more!

What is your favourite dressing-up costume?

Ideas:

Flowers	Clown
Stripes	Cave girl
Animal	Magician
Stars	Nurse
Superhero	

Who Wants To Play

Do you like to play music? Make your own trumpet like Little Princess. Then play music concerts for everyone in the castle.

You will need:

Cardboard toilet paper tube
Yellow or gold paper
Scissors
Glue
3 buttons

Get ready to get messy!
Ask a grown-up to help with tricky parts and wear an apron.

Instructions:

1. Draw two funnel shapes onto yellow or gold paper. The long part should be the same length as the cardboard tube.

2. Ask a grown-up to help you to cut them out.

3. Glue the two funnel shapes around the cardboard tube.

4. Glue the top and bottom of the funnel together to make a horn shape.

5. Glue three buttons on the top.

Little Princess's
Royal Reward Chart

This chart belongs to

Date

Make your bed
M T W T F

Put away your toys
M T W T F

Brush your teeth
M T W T F

Comb your hair
M T W T F

M T W T F

M T W T F

M T W T F

M T W T F

This week I...

Use the unmarked boxes to put your own family actions. For example, feeding the animals, laying the table, doing a good turn etc.

I Want To Recycle

Little Princess was drawing in her bedroom when she realised her bowl of ice cream had melted.

"I'll go and get some more," she decided.

She went to the kitchen.

"Chef, can I have some more ice cream, please?" asked Little Princess. "Mine's gone all gooey."

"Ah non, it has all gone, every last dollop," replied Chef.

Little Princess was very disappointed.

King and Queen were playing croquet outside.

"Can I have some more drawing paper?" asked Little Princess.

"We're all out," replied King.

"But we've run out of everything!" Little Princess complained.

Queen smiled. "That's why it's important not to waste things, sweetheart," she said.

"When you waste paper, more trees have to be cut down," added King.

"Trees?" asked Little Princess.

"Paper comes from trees," explained King. "They chop them down."

"Chop them down!" cried Little Princess. "Poor trees! I'm not going to waste paper or other stuff ever again."

Little Princess found lots of things that would normally be thrown away in the royal bins. She piled everything into her pram.

"La-la-la, I'm not wasting anything!" she sang.

Little Princess found an old tyre by the shed, but it was too heavy for her to pick up.

"Allow me!" smiled General, popping out from behind the shed.

He huffed and puffed, and finally dropped the tyre into the pram.

"Goodness, you've got a lot of things," exclaimed General. "Are you going to recycle them?"

Little Princess thought for a moment. "What's RE-CY-CLE?"

"It's turning things that aren't wanted any more into new things," General explained.

Little Princess decided that recycling sounded fun. First she decided to recycle the old bucket she had found.

"Here you are, Horace," she beamed. "A drinks bucket!"

She didn't notice that all the water leaked out again.

Next Little Princess recycled an old box into a house for Puss and Scruff. It didn't work very well. They bumped into Chef as he carried a cake.

Little Princess grabbed the box.

"I'll recycle this again," she said.

Little Princess kept thinking of ways to recycle all the things she had saved from being wasted.

"Maybe Admiral would like this tyre as a new swimming ring," she said.

She spun the tyre so fast that it flew down the stairs, through the front door, over the vegetable patch and hit two apple trees. CRASH!

Little Princess looked at all the apples on the ground.

"Now I have even more stuff to recycle!" she said.

Little Princess went to her bedroom to sulk.

"Nobody wants the things I give them," she said.

She thought hard, and then she got up.

"I'm giving them the wrong things," she said. "I know what to do."

"Chef, would you like something nice from my pram?" Little Princess asked. "You can choose anything you want."

"Ah oui, I would love these apples to make puddings galore!" he replied.

"Hello Gardener," called Little Princess. "Would you like to choose something from my pram?"

Gardener chose the re-recycled box to store all his empty flowerpots.

"Thank you," he said with a chuckle.

"Would you like anything from my pram?" Little Princess asked King and Queen.

"That bucket will be just right for my croquet balls," said King.

Little Princess pushed off her pram singing a new song.

"I love recycling!"

"I'm very good at recycling now," Little Princess said happily. "I've recycled almost everything."

She looked at what was left in her pram.

"Would anyone like a nice piece of rope?" she bellowed. "Or a lovely tyre?"

Little Princess saw Algie on the swing.

"Come and play," he called. "I'm on the swing first."

"But that's my swing," huffed Little Princess.

Suddenly she had another recycling idea and asked King to help her.

"Ta-da!" said King.

He presented Little Princess with her new swing. It was made from the recycled tyre and piece of rope.

"Wow, thank you," she said.

Chef brought a recycled treat too.

"Here are two delicious milkshakes made from your melted ice cream," he said.

Little Princess giggled.

"Recycling is fun and yummy!"

Make Your Own
Desk Tidy

You can do your own bit of royal recycling and make a castle desk tidy from old cardboard tubes.

Get ready to get messy!
Ask a grown-up to help with cutting and wear an apron.

Instructions:

1. Ask a grown-up to cut two of the cardboard tubes in half.
2. Turn the shoebox lid upside down and paint the inside green.
3. Paint all the cardboard tubes purple inside and out.
4. Wait for the tubes to dry.
5. With the black pen, draw turrets, windows and bricks on the outside of the painted cardboard tubes.
6. Make 6 small cuts in the bottom of the cardboard tubes. Cuts should be 1cm deep
7. Glue the cardboard tubes onto the shoebox lid. The four half tubes should be in the centre and the four taller ones on the corners.
8. Fold the rectangle of paper in half and glue together with the drinking straw into the centre.
9. Draw a crown on each side and stick it in the middle to look like the flag on top of the castle.

Use your recycled desk tidy to keep all your crayons and pencils together.

Did you know?

There are lots of ways you can recycle:

1. Use both sides of your drawing paper.
2. Wash and reuse food containers.
3. Turn old food into compost for the garden.

Admiral's Pond Puzzler

Did you know? Admiral has a pet frog called Hornpipe. Can you spot him?

Admiral has written a secret water message for you.

Have you seen any sea monsters?

Hold this page up to a mirror to reveal Admiral's message.

Algie's Brainteaser Challenge

Cheeky Algie is always asking Little Princess riddles. Can you help her to work out the answers to the questions below?

1. What belongs to you but others use it more than you do?

2. What has four fingers and one thumb, but is not alive?

3. What is full of holes, but can still hold a lot of water?

Try out some of Algie's jokes on your friends and family:

Q: Why did the lion spit out the clown?

A: Because he tasted funny!

Q: How can you tell the sea is friendly?

A: Because it waves!

The A to Z of

Aa is for Algie, Little Princess's cheeky friend.

Bb is for bike. One way Little Princess likes to get around the castle.

Cc is for Chef. Chef makes yummy treats.

Dd is for Desmond, Little Princess's inflatable crocodile.

Ee is for explorer. Little Princess loves to explore.

Ff is for flag. This flag flies from the top of the castle.

Gg is for Gilbert, Little Princess's favourite teddy bear.

Little Princess

There is a lot to learn from the Little Princess, her friends and the castle.
Here is the A-Z of what there is to see. Write over the dotty letters as you go.

Hh is for Horace. Horace is a very stubborn Shetland pony.

Ii is for ice cream, , Little Princess's favourite dessert.

Jj is for jelly. Chef makes the wobbliest jelly.

Kk is for King, Little Princess's dad.

Ll is for lilo, somewhere comfy to sit on the beach.

Mm is for Maid. Maid keeps everything clean in the castle.

Nn is for Nessie, General's trusty hobbyhorse.

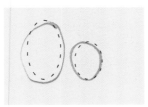 is for owl. Little Princess knows it's bedtime when she hears "tu-whit-tu-whoo."

 is for Puss. Puss is a very clever cat.

 is for Queen, Little Princess's mum.

 is for rubber ring. Admiral always has his rubber ring close at hand.

 is for Scruff. Scruff is a very loyal dog.

is for tree house. Little Princess's favourite den.

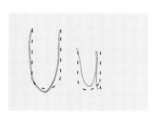 is for umbrella. Umbrellas are useful on rainy days.

 is for vegetables. Gardener likes to grow lots and lots of vegetables!

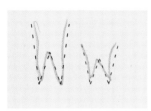 is for Walter. Great Uncle Walter always livens up the castle.

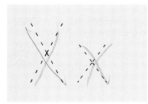 is for 'X' marks the spot on King's treasure map.

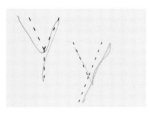 is for "yummy". Little Princess's favourite dinner is yummy sausages.

is for zoom! Prime Minister loves to zoom around on his tricycle.

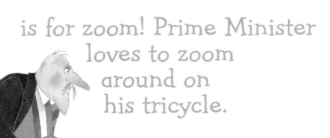

Colouring
Fairground

Little Princess is going to the fair. There's a big wheel, a bouncy castle and even a merry-go-round! Use crayons or pencils to colour in all the exciting rides.

Use bright colours to make it extra fun!

My Best

Little Princess has lots of favourite things. Her favourite teddy is Gilbert. Her best friend is Algie. She loves to dress up and explore.

Use the spaces to write about things that you like.

My favourite colour …

My favourite teddy bear …

My best friend …

My pet …

My favourite game …

My favourite food …

Things

My favourite place ...

Choose your favourite season:

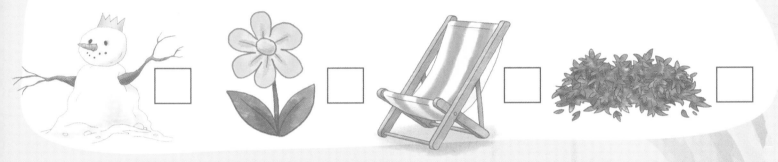

My Treasure

Draw what you would hide in your treasure chest.

Suppertime squares

King and Queen are playing a game after supper.
You and a friend can play too.

1. Ask a friend to play. Choose who will be Queen and who will be King.

2. Take it in turns to draw a line connecting any two dots. No diagonals, though!

3. Try to make a four-sided square. The player who finishes the square puts their initial inside. (K for King or Q for Queen)

4. When there are no more dots left, count the letters.

5. The player with the most boxes wins!

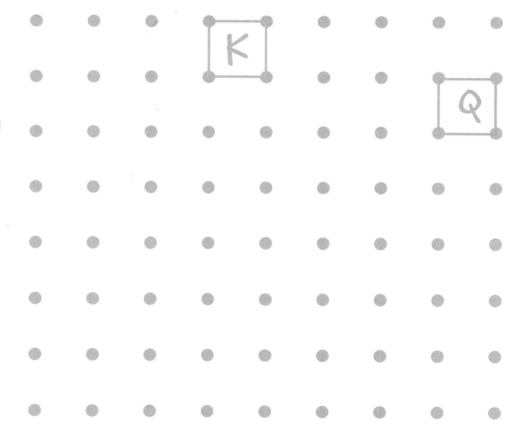

Castle Close-ups

It's bedtime at the castle and everyone is wearing nightclothes.
Can you work out whose nightclothes are shown in the pictures below?
Draw a line to match the close-ups with the right person.

Little Princess and her friends have had lots of fun with you. They hope that you have enjoyed your Little Princess Annual! Use crayons or pencils to colour them in one last time.

Colouring:
Little Princess with Gilbert, Puss and Scruff

Answers

Page 6

There are 4 squirrels, 4 candy canes and 5 clockwork mice.

Page 15

There are 5 presents.

Page 28

1 – A, 2 – B, 3 – D, 4 – C, 5 – E

Page 29

1. Algie 2. ice cream 3. DOLL appears 3 times

Page 30

Rubber rings C and H match.

Page 34

K	Y	K	J	U	M	P	E	R	V
N	V	E	S	I	N	P	Y	S	B
I	S	S	Y	D	L	T	S	H	E
C	O	P	H	R	S	R	M	I	L
K	C	S	V	E	E	L	T	R	U
E	K	E	V	S	E	H	U	T	C
R	S	U	U	S	G	T	S	T	T
S	R	O	E	I	B	Q	A	A	G
V	R	Q	N	I	N	X	D	C	Y
T	F	D	T	X	R	C	Q	V	Q

Page 40

Algie leads to the cake

Page 41

There are 3 white rabbits.

Page 55

Scruff stole the biscuits.

Page 56-57

Page 59

3 balls and 1 bear = 4.

There are 2 planes and 3 boats. There are 5 toys altogether.

You need to add two crayons.

Page 62

Puzzle piece number 2 is the missing piece.

Page 63

Page 80

Admiral's message says:
Have you seen any sea monsters?
The frog is on the wooden jetty.

Page 81

1. Your name
2. A glove.
3. A sponge.

Page 91

1 –E, 2 – B, 3 – A,
4 – D, 5 – C